Copyright 2007 by Bill Glose
All Rights Reserved
Manufactured in the United States of America

Editor: Robert P. Arthur
Designer: Jeff Hewitt

San Francisco Bay Press
1671 39th Street
San Francisco, California 94122

SFP Paperback Edition
Library of Congress Cataloguing in
Publication Data

Glose, Bill: The Human Touch

ISBN Number 978-1-60461-000-0

THE HUMAN TOUCH

Poems

By Bill Glose

The Human Touch
- Spencer Michael Free
1856-1938

'Tis the human touch in this world that counts,
The touch of your hand and mine,
Which means far more to the fainting heart
Than shelter and bread and wine;
For shelter is gone when the night is o'er,
And bread lasts only a day,
But the touch of the hand and the sound of the voice
Sing on in the soul alway.

Grateful acknowledgements are due to the editors of the following publications where these poems have appeared, sometimes in slightly different form or under different titles:

Artemis Journal: "Plugged In," originally published as "Filters and Screens"

BaySplash: "Chesapeake Vision" and "Living on Graph Paper"

The Blotter: "Springtime for the Disinclined"

Bound: "Hurricane Memories"

Chrysanthemum: "Memories of St. Tropez"

Far West End Press: "A Perfect Day"

Main Channel Voices: "End of the World"

Main Street Rag: "Keeping Appointments"

The Poet's Domain: "A Lesson from my Dogs"

Port Folio Weekly: "Cutting Hair," originally published as "Cutting"

Red Pepper: "Such a Nice Boy"

Red River Review: "An Empty Bed" and "Ride"

Sabella: "A Perfect Day," "Release," and "Through My Window"

Virginia Adversaria: "Plugged In," published as "Filters and Screens"

Special thanks are due to Ann Shalaski for her critical eye and sharp pen; to Nancy Powell, whose tireless work and enthusiasm as *Virginia Adversaria's* Poetry Editor provided inspiration; and to Carolyn Kreiter-Foronda, for her gracious heart and influence.

The Human Touch
Table of Contents

PRELUDE

Vision of the Future	1

DROWNING IN SUBURBIA

Living on Graph Paper	5
Plugged In	6
Casting Stones	7
Midnight Diversion	8
Chesapeake Vision	9
When I Think About the Hurricane	10
Memories of St. Tropez	12
Fishing with my Son	13
Into the Earth	14
Ride	17
A Lesson from my Dogs	18
Rejection Slips	19

TASTE OF SATURDAY NIGHT

A Perfect Day	23
Billy Collins	24
Time Traveling	25
Elegy to a Kiss	26
Cutting Hair	27
Chasing Butterflies	28
Through My Window	29

Circular Logic   30
End of the World   32
A Father's Love   33
Keeping Appointments   34

THE WEIGHT OF WINTER

Yard Sales   39
Fathers and Sons   40
Magnitude   41
Rodin   42
Man with an Upright Bass   43
Love is not Haiku   44
An Empty Bed   45
Learning to Cry   46
Springtime for the Disinclined   47
Release   48
I Wish   49
Such a Nice Boy   50
Hurricane Memories   51

for my parents

PRELUDE

Vision of the Future

Amid the frolic of giggling children
is an old man sequestered on a park bench,

his loneliness a linen suit, creases
crisp as creeping moan of evening.

Nannies cast suspicious stares, steer charges away
while paper-thin teens in sagging shorts

point, laugh, know age will never sink claws
into them. Wary pigeons peck

at breadcrumbs he tosses like lost years.
My daughter, 6, spins circles in a field

of purple phlox, yellow Easter dress belling
like a tulip, strawberry hair wild, white stockings

smudged green at the knees. Ten years from now
when I hear the creak of a windowsill betraying

a foot sneaking outside, I hope I trust the sweetness
of her heart, think of today, see her approach the bench,

a ladybug in cupped hands cracked open
for rheumy eyes filled with wonder,

spring blooming on a face
lost in winter far too long.

DROWNING IN SUBURBIA

Living on Graph Paper

No one writes poems about subdivisions,
about the grid of privacy fences
delineating one symmetrical lawn
from another. No one commemorates
lives lived on graph paper, the joyful
absence of free will, the pleasure
of passing years on schedule,
tap-tap-tapping
to someone else's
metronome.

No one celebrates the way
homogenized living turns you
into a child at the pool—no running,
no splashing, no horseplay—where
the lifeguard is too concerned
with consistency of zinc
on his nose to notice you sinking,
trying to breathe underwater,
pressure building
like a slowly
squeezing
fist.

Instead, poets use pens to carve
up condo rules, cannonball
into the pool, swim outside
float-marked lanes and
splash water in the face
of anyone who tries to corral
them, kicking free in a way
that evokes primordial ancestors
struggling for shore
to find
a place
to breathe.

Plugged In

In the fortress of his basement,
physical company comes only
from dust motes swirling
between cinderblocks,
fluorescence dimly aping
the light his skin yearns for.

Scuttling to a window, his face
fists into a mole's grimace.
On the other side of the blinds
he is more transparent
than bits and bytes in a line
of code, but downstairs

the world is filled with
smiley faces and LOL's,
a chat room icon
declares him demi-god,
and anything is possible
with just a point and click.

Casting Stones

On TV, victims wade
through flooded streets clutching
bottled water and dry food; a few
carry electronic equipment,
beer and cigarettes.

He judges from an overstuffed chair,
ensconced in air-conditioning,
bag of chips and soda at his side.
"Damn looters," he says. "Shoot them all."

Hurricane relief numbers scroll by
and he snorts at the thought; his cash
is earmarked for more important things—
a new Game Boy cartridge,
designer jeans from The Gap.

He changes channels to
his favorite show, where contestants
eat pureed insects and dangle from helicopters.
"What idiots," he says, imagining
all the while what he would do
with the prize money
if he were on the show
and won.

Midnight Diversion

Another weekend conference cuts short
    time I treasure, time off the clock,
    when I pretend paychecks and
    bosses hold no sway over life.

Sneaking from a hotel bed, I slip into
    loose and roomy trunks,
    freed from starched shirts
    and ties that strangle the kid in me.

In darkness, I pad down the hall,
    eloping with the playful spirit that
    sat quietly through business meetings,
    biding time till we could be alone.

With impish grin, he begs me to play,
    come outside where salt air
    tickles my nose and beach breeze
    runs fingers through my hair.

Crashing waves call out, cool sand
    soothes cramped toes. Running
    and skipping, I leap into surf,
    splash water at the sky, refuse to grow old.

Chesapeake Vision

When I stand on Tidewater's marshy shore,
my back turned to the modern world,
it's easy to pretend I am the first man
to set foot in this space, so faultless and pure.
Wind sighs through sawgrass, carries the scent
of salt and pine. Clouds tumble overhead,
bits of fluff that frolic through
an amber sky. The sun tucks into
the distant shore, its skyline natural,
free from progress. Day's last light
turns rippling water into liquid gold
and streaks the sky with colors
I didn't know existed.

I wonder if this is how John Smith felt
gazing across Chesapeake Bay for
the first time, standing on a spot
like this. If he could cast ahead
400 years and witness the impact
of civilization, would he still yearn
to tame the wilderness, to build
and colonize and conquer? Or
would he linger but one day
to marvel at the boundless beauty
before setting sail to leave
this land unspoiled?

When I Think About the Hurricane

I remember swollen tides,
snapped power lines, fallen trees,
people sifting through ruined homes,
stacking detritus by the road,
crying over keepsakes
pulled from rain-soaked drawers.

In the odd stillness
we blinked away sitcom stupors,
gathered with neighbors whose
names we didn't know,
shared blankets and bottled water,
gave words of comfort.

We cleared debris from
each other's yards,
pulled limbs from roofs,
sawed trunks of giant pines,
tired of holding up the sky,
now reposed on our lawns.

At night we'd pull
a crescent of lawn chairs
around a generator,
grill hot dogs together,
our children racing
in the fading twilight.

But what I remember most
when I think about the hurricane
is sitting in my foyer one month later,
a bowl of candy on my lap,
waiting for superheroes
and goblins, witches
and magicians
who never
appeared,
their magic
used up.

Memories of St. Tropez

It is just a sweatshirt,
worn thin at the elbows,
dun-colored like coarse,
Carolina sand, not fine,
white silt of the Riviera,
whose bright emblems
displayed on the chest
promise color to all who visit.

Before the neck and cuffs
stretched into droopy cowls,
it was your favorite
for morning runs, evening walks,
or lying in bed, my hand
crawling underneath to trace
the arc of your ribs,
feel your heart.

When you exchanged it for
business suits, watching CNN
on motel beds with hospital corners,
I'd settle in our loveseat,
wear your shirt like a tent,
knees folded inside as a faraway
clerk took my messages.

But these days, when I pull it from
a drawer and try to sniff memory
from the weathered fabric,
I see that day in Wilmington,
aluminum legs of our beach chairs
tucked into the sand. You held
my hand and said, Close your eyes,
imagine you're in St. Tropez.

Fishing with my Son

When I was young my father
took me to the farm
where he grew up to teach
me how to fish. We grubbed
the marshy shore for worms,
cast them on the water,
tickling lines back to shore
in hopes lake creatures would leap
into our waiting hands.
We caught nothing more
than sun on our shoulders,
mud in our boots; what we
brought home, though, weighed
more than any trophy fish, lives
longer than the age of water itself.

Twenty years later, I packed my son
into a car, drove to my first apartment
in a complex, I recalled being different
than those surrounding it—
a park at its heart, a walking path
circling a pond. I brought tackle boxes,
store-bought lures, rods with reels
still sealed in plastic. We found
a golf course where the park once stood.
My son used the landing net to
chase frogs into a ditch, and I promised
he could keep one as a pet,
hoping his memory would be brighter
than the bulldozed truth.

Into the Earth

I.

As traffic inches toward
the tunnel, road signs warn
of delays, blinking to a tune
of angry horns. A smoky blanket
covers the bruised sky, blots out
the sun. Steel-gray water
chops at bridge piers, sending
seagulls squalling like
sibling children confined
to back seats, unaware
they might one day
look back on their
vacation with fondness.

II.

My mind dips into yesteryear
where I curl in a heap
with sisters, dozing
to engine's hum, rhythmic
vibration of tires on pavement.
My father's hand—giant, firm,
not yet affected by tremors or
blotched with spots—reaches
from the front, shakes us awake,
points to the approaching tunnel,
tells us it's a giant's mouth
stretched wide to swallow
us whole. Seagulls wheel overhead,
dip low to glide beside us,
an escort for the sacrifice,
breaking off just before we
descend into the earth.

III.

In those invincible days,
how cheated I felt that someone
so giant and firm could fall
to an illness I couldn't pronounce,
be gone a year from diagnosis.
So cheated I couldn't cry
at the funeral, stored tears
in the well of my heart,
deeper than a gravedigger's
pit. How strange that now,
approaching the tunnel,
they should rise in buckets,
spill on my shirt,
speak the farewell
my lips were
never able.

Ride

On weekends I would fly
with Daddy in his '66 Vette,
soaring past pedestrians,
engine screaming and my hand
flapping roller coaster tracks in the wind,
while Dad's Izods
smoothly shifted gears
and patted my leg.

Now, instead of sitting
in his sleek sportster,
I ride in a grand car that creeps so slowly
my outstretched fingers cannot fly.
Bystanders turn grave faces downward
and there's no gloved hand
to pat my knee
or wipe away Mom's tears.

A Lesson From My Dogs

When I encounter
well-meaning friends
who boast of success,
offer career advice, suggest
alternatives to writing,
I ask my dogs,
the reasons why.

"Do you ever worry," I say,
"what other dogs think, wonder
which ones growl behind
your back? Do you crave
better chew toys, designer food
from a can? Ever wish
you were something else?"

They pant and wag till
I snap on leashes,
open the door, then
they sprint outside,
towing me behind.

There's a whiff of something
on the breeze;
they must investigate,
sniff and run,
be what they were meant to be.

Rejection Slips

Why, when you polish your words to perfection,
does the mail dare to bring you another rejection?

You expected acceptance, a contract, and glory,
or a call from an agent who was wowed by your story

about terrorists on steroids cloning monkeys that sing—
how could anyone say no to such a sure thing?

The plot was so topical, and the last time you checked
your writing was on par with Ernest Steinbeck.

Your manuscript must not have been read to the end
where everything is explained as the spaceship descends.

Stop ranting you fool; you can moan, whine, and pout,
but fight fire with fire and you're sure to win out.

If they can refuse to accept what you sent,
I say do the same and see if they'll relent.

Reject their rejection with a slip of your own,
something tacky, generic, bureaucratic in tone.

Don't address your reply to a person by name,
"Whom it concerns" or "Dear Sir" will do just the same.

Be sure to bemoan how difficult your plight:
you can't give them more time, it just wouldn't be right

to the other editors who sent a rejection;
sheer volume prevents individual attention.

But feel free, you must add, to reject me again,
just send at the right time, for it does matter when.

My reading period is brief, I'm sorry to say,
it's open from never till the fourth of no way.

TASTE OF SATURDAY NIGHT

A Perfect Day

Today is a perfect day,
though I woke up late
forgot to shave,
and hit each red light
going to work.

Today is a perfect day,
not 'cause I won pick-six lotto
(no numbers matched)
or got the deli's last pie
(all were gone).

Today is a perfect day,
because last night
you kissed me,
and the taste of you lingers,
hinting at the promise of tonight.

Billy Collins

My lover wishes I were Billy Collins,
that I could shape words with his carefree
elegance, describe the beauty of her face,
her eyes, not mentioning, of course,
bifocal lenses or crow's feet
caused by squinting
from not wearing aforementioned
glasses. She'd like me to pen lyrical
couplets that praise the sculpture
of her body, shaving off excess pounds
she always talks about losing,
smoothing out cellulite, lifting
anything that sags. She wants me to craft
a poem that's clever yet deep, passionate
yet thoughtful, spontaneous yet rhythmic;
she wants this though I am a mere limerick
among sonnets, fumbling with words
that spill gracefully from other mouths;

she wants this
        but settles for me instead.

Time Traveling

They say gazing at stars
is like time traveling,
light reaching our eyes
from distant nebulae
that may, by now, no longer
exist. The radiance
they emit navigates
an ocean of space
over millions of years,
showing up on Earth to
play a part in our cosmic show,
one point in a constellation's
connect-the-dot pattern or
a bright and solitary pinprick
in the universe's
velveteen fabric.

That's how it is
when I look in your
face; instead of
blots and wrinkles
earned from a life
well spent, the image
I see comes to me from
years ago. I gaze
back in time
at a person who
saw the future,
convinced me
to be deeper than
superficial swagger,
captured my heart,
still holds it
in her hands.

Elegy to a Kiss

I think when you are gone
the thing I will miss most
is the feel of your lips
on mine, taste of memory
they provide. Each time
we kiss, I relive the others—
from the clumsy first to
playful last, a million
tender brushes, lusty nibbles,
and perfunctory pecks
in-between. And if I am
first to go then know
the lick of wind that
tickles your neck hairs
on morning walks
is the kiss I'm blowing
you from Heaven.

Cutting Hair

I sit still on a straight-backed chair
in the center of the kitchen,
a flowered sheet draped over my shoulders
fastened at my neck with a clothespin.

You nudge my neck forward,
fingers skimming my scalp,
tugging tufts of hair to equal lengths
while snipping scissors silence
echoes of last night's argument.

It is always like this—you,
bridging sullen divides without words;
me, quietly accepting the grace of your touch,
thankful you can take that step.

I wish I could, too,
but I was never good
with scissors.

Chasing Butterflies

The ballet has gone on since dawn
—longer—roles scripted in genes.
She's the graceful butterfly, vibrant,
enticing; he, the hunter, confident, strong,
lured by her rhythm, lumbering in
her rainbow contrail with a clumsy net.

How clever she is, though,
deftly dancing out of reach
while desire climbs its peak
before slyly settling on a leaf,
never betraying surprise
at her capture, letting him believe
their union had something
to do with his choice.

Through My Window

You blow through my dreams,
a rose-scented breeze
with a hint of jasmine,

swirling like
a jumble of leaves
caught in a whirlwind,

spinning
       teasing
              calling

urging me to leap,
ride the wind
out my window

escape through fluttering
curtains into night,
where we can dance forever
in the starry sky.

Circular Logic

In the early days of infatuation
when the world has more texture,
tastes better, looks brighter,
when I feel smarter and sexier
than anyone has a right to be,

I can't help
wondering
if this will last.

It's the circular logic you hear
on talk shows—abused sons
who grow to beat their wives,
their children; or the women
who seek them out, one hitter
after another.

Experience illustrates love's course—
a tornado that springs from nowhere,
spins the world as a carousel, pulls you
into its vortex then moves on,
leaving wreckage in its wake.

Or it can remain, slowly losing strength,
carrying you to the land where
married friends reside, bitter
from biding time through cold
and silent winters, the tempest
that threw them together long forgotten.

Perhaps, too, there is a third option,
one that defies history—a belief
that an optimistic heart can overcome
any obstacle, even the prejudice
of its own mind,

a hope that keeps
fools like me
falling in love.

End of the World

If the world were about to end
and I could be with one woman
for that final eve,

I'd spend those hours
with the woman I abandoned
in wild days of my youth,

when everything tasted like Saturday night
and I hadn't yet learned that
love is more important than lust.

I'd come to her after all these years,
kiss her crows feet and age spots,
bend an ear to her lips,

hoping she'd whisper forgiveness
so I could close my eyes
and greet forever with a smile.

A Father's Love

for his son can never equal
that for a daughter, though
he'll profess it to be. She is
simply too foreign a creature,
clomping to a mirror in a pair
of her mother's heels, turning
pirouettes in a bubble-gum pink
tutu. She'll change his calloused
idea of what it means to be strong
into something soft as rose petals,
delicate as a kitten's neck.

When she trades Barbie posters
for long-haired rock stars, paints
her lips into bright promises
for smirking boys, he'll clutch
the teddy bear she hasn't
yet discarded, recall her dancing
in her mother's shoes, frozen
like the hands of a grandfather
clock he refuses to wind.

Keeping Appointments

For years I punched a factory timecard
to account for every second. Breaks
were twenty minutes—never twenty-one—
and late to work meant someone
suffered in your stead, for no machine
could be unattended. Now I live
among creative folk, poets and artists
who view clocks in the abstract,
something scribed in verse or
brushed into a Dali landscape.
They laugh at appointments, arrive
ten minutes past whenever, say
the sky was a shade of blue
never seen before and to rush away
without reflection would be an injustice
to the sweetness of living.

THE WEIGHT OF WINTER

Yard Sales

There's something sad about a yard sale
that prevents me from stopping. Even the
cardboard sign is forlorn, tacked
lopsided to a telephone pole,
directing scavengers, who descend
on the carcass to rip and tear in search
of vitals. Once-precious relics strewn atop
folding tables convey certainty that anything
may one day be unwelcome, relegated
to the dark, swaddled in dust
instead of affection. It's where I expect
to find myself some day, in a bargain bin
scratching foolscap with a fountain pen,
crafting poems for a society that wants
nothing more than sitcoms.

Fathers and Sons

Fathers should never die
before they are grandfathers,
when sons most need
guidance, wisdom;
when, seeing through
parent's eyes, their
world transforms
in the blink of birth
to one brighter than
a rainbow, sharper
than cut glass.

Fathers should never die
before their boys are men
who can fit but one
calloused finger
in the clasp of a tiny hand,
muscle and steel
softened by the velvet
of a baby's crown.

Fathers should never die
before sons thank them
for life lessons, say
"I love you"
before a funeral
requires it, when
farewells flutter
like so many petals
down a hole
in the damp Earth.

Magnitude
— for Terry

Friday nights we gather at
a Mexican restaurant
to whine about failed diets,
traffic jams, noisy kids,
mundane events we carry
like stones in otherwise
uneventful lives, wishing
for something — anything —
to scatter the span
of similar days.

Until it does. Until,
one day, one of us
discovers a lump
in her breast, comes
to dinner with blue targets
tattooed on her sternum,
in her armpit, waits
for flesh to be cut,
chemicals to drip
through veins.

The mass — a mere dot
on a mammogram
X-ray — is large enough
to place normalcy
in past tense,
something we crave
and can't regain
no matter how
many margaritas
we sip.

Rodin
– for Dawn

He was just a parrot I didn't love,
or even like that much. My girlfriend's
pet. He would serenade her, whistle
in his throat, speak bits of chatter,
but for me would only squawk,
scream "Murder, murder." I'd feed
and water him when she was away.
Rodin would bite my fingers,
aching to carve flesh like his
sculptor namesake, calloused beak
unable to effect damage his
hateful eyes hoped to see.

I sometimes thought of opening
the door, inviting a neighbor's cat
to visit, or leaving windows cracked,
enough so Rodin could flap
into woods, where spiteful
comments would be silenced
by creatures unsympathetic
to the way he perched on another's
shoulder, sang of jealous love,
brought joy to her face.

When he started pulling feathers
from an already threadbare coat,
my girlfriend said, "He's preparing
to die." On the last day, she held
him in her palm, stroked his spine.
I dug a hole behind her house,
laid him inside while a nearby stream
burbled a eulogy, our moment of silence
pierced by a Bob-white rudely
yapping his refrain, saying goodbye
to an old and crotchety relative.

Man with an Upright Bass

In the back of a bluegrass band
stands a man with an upright bass,
hugging the instrument by her waist
like a lover, nuzzling the spiraling scroll
of her neck as if whispering a secret
that vibrates in her heart, escapes
through f-shaped sound holes.
Others spin bull fiddles like tops,
slap salt and pepper gut on fingerboards,
climb ribs with frenzied antics; his
rough fingers coax melody from
steel strings in a dim corner where
the spotlight never ventures, maple gloss
of his lover's belly and rounded shoulders
meant for no one but him.

The world spins to his rhythm, taps toes
to his beat, but turns its eye to the
slender girl bouncing a tambourine
on her hip, midriff bare, skirt flaring,
bosom straining skintight cotton.
Too beautiful, she sings of tragic love
she cannot understand. Partners embrace,
sway in slow circles on a dance floor.
Only the bassist and those who hide
in darkened corners, clasping
half-filled glasses for company,
comprehend the lyrics
of unrequited love.

Love is not Haiku

At breakfast she says,
"I don't love you anymore,"
her face calm, composed.

I can't ask questions
that thunder inside my head
and rattle my teeth.

But how can it end
when my feelings haven't changed,
and I'm still in love?

She grabs a suitcase,
throws in clothes and underwear,
leaves pictures behind—

framed wedding photos,
the "till death do us part" smiles
now collecting dust.

From the door, I watch,
count her steps down the brick path,
into the taxi,

hear the door snap shut,
the engine rev and tires squeal.
She never looks back.

An Empty Bed

No one is there
when I wake,
no hand on my back
or hip pressing mine,
only the weight
of swelling silence.

Sweaty sheets knot
around my knees—
an anchor to keep me
from well-meaning friends
who bludgeon with pity,
stab with soundless stares.

Stroking the vacant space,
my fingers remember
tickling your ribs,
lips recall taste
of your neck, ears
mourn lost music,

pillow talk
swallowed by
an empty bed
filled with absence,
forever passing in night
as seconds tick away.

Learning to Cry

"Learn to cry,"
you often said.
And I'd reply,
"I can't, I'm a man."
And so you went,
leaving your pillow
for me to stain
with my tears.

Springtime for the Disinclined

It must be spring again—
I hear the birds twittering
outside my window
cooing and cheeping till
I want to claw my eyes out.

Calls to codes compliance
won't shut them up
like it did my neighbors
with their outdoor parties
and teenage boys,

who even now
are spraying dad's car
before they take it
on a double date
with Barbie bubble-heads,

or worse yet,
plan to bring them home
to romp and giggle
in the yard,

unmindful of those
who only wish for
the sequestered silence
of winter.

Release

Shuffling over slick streets,
I carry the beast
to a dark destination.
It paces inside,
yearning to escape,
clawing my skin.

Troubled mothers
shield their babes
while others gawk
beneath bent brows.
Unasked questions fill the air
until I pass and
happy thoughts return.

Inside a blackened room,
I find release
instead of pity.
The needle pricks my skin
and the beast roars through my veins,
consuming me.

I become my animal self—
a lemming—
scampering toward a cliff,
and when I leap
for one
       exultant
              moment,
I fly.

I Wish

Sometimes when you yell at me
so hard the pulsing vein in your neck
threatens to burst through your skin,

I wish you'd shrink
to how small you
make me feel.

Then maybe I'd find
the courage to step down
and crush you with my heel,

walk barefoot out the door,
strolling through grass that wipes
your stain from my soul.

Such a Nice Boy

After the last victim falls
and he turns the gun
on himself,

neighbors will daub makeup
and pose for cameras,
wearing their shock
like a garnish.

With trembling voice they'll say,
"He was such a nice boy,"
wide eyes and O-shaped mouths
perfect for news-at-ten sound bites,

though later, as they twist in their sheets,
they'll wonder if tonight,
for the first time in years,
sleep will be peaceful,

or if they'll see his face again.

Hurricane Memories

Funny how for years I'd pass by,
never slowing, though it was once
a weekly occurrence, a necessity.
Time was we'd opt for dinner there
instead of making it ourselves,
or simply stop for a beer, or two.
You'd comment on the bright
uniforms, red and white
striped jerseys adorned with
eclectic pins as strange a mix
as our relationship.

Sitting in our booth once more
I salivate over memories instead of
entrees displayed on placards,
savor your smile, full and bright,
frequently given; your hair,
shimmering like pond-reflected light;
your scent, faint strawberries
that lingered weeks
on sheets you left behind.

Hurrying home to my efficiency,
I see your curly script
in my address book,
"I Love You" written in the margins;
in a flash, the other memories come back,
tempestuous ones swirling outside
the calm eye of sentiment, stormy
ones that urge me to move on.

Gently I finger your name,
caress the thought of you.
Ignoring another sitcom featuring
happy-ending families
I reach for the phone, a lifeboat
bobbing in my hurricane past
begging me to climb aboard.

About the Author

Born into an Air Force family in California, Bill Glose spent most of his childhood hopping around different bases overseas—Japan, then Okinawa, then England. In 1979, his father was stationed at Langley Air Force Base in Hampton Roads, and ever since Bill has called Virginia his home.

He joined ROTC at Virginia Tech in hopes of becoming a fighter pilot like his father. His eyes weren't good enough, so he joined the 82d Airborne instead. If he couldn't fly the planes, he figured he'd jump out of them. His father still can't understand why anyone would jump out of a perfectly good airplane.

After five years as a paratrooper and commanding a platoon in combat, Bill moved on to manufacturing. He was a line supervisor in a Chicago factory and then a plant manager in Massachusetts. His military and factory backgrounds have greatly influenced his writing, as evidenced by "Keeping Appointments" in this collection and "Collateral Damage" in *Hello, Goodbye*.

Bill's prose and poetry have appeared in *GRIT*, *Main Channel Voices*, *Red River Press*, *The Summerset Review*, and numerous other markets. Honors include the 2001 F. Scott Fitzgerald Short Story Award and the 2004 Virginia Press Association First Place Award for Sports News Writing. When he is not writing his regular column for *Virginia Living*, freelancing, or writing for himself, he's probably watching a movie or a Hokie football game.

More information is available online at www.BillGlose.com.

MAIN
LOCAL AUTHOR

Made in the USA